YOU ARE
A STORY

BOB RACZKA

PICTURES BY
KRISTEN AND **KEVIN**
HOWDESHELL

NEAL PORTER BOOKS
HOLIDAY HOUSE / NEW YORK

Neal Porter Books

Text copyright © 2023 by Bob Raczka
Illustrations copyright © 2023 by Brave Union, LLC
All Rights Reserved
HOLIDAY HOUSE is registered in the U.S. Patent and Trademark Office.
Printed and bound in March 2024 by C&C Offset, Shenzhen, China.
The artwork for this book was created with Adobe Photoshop.
Book design by Jennifer Browne
www.holidayhouse.com
First Edition
3 5 7 9 10 8 6 4

Library of Congress Cataloging-in-Publication Data is available.

ISBN: 978-0-8234-4914-9 (hardcover)

To Emma —B.R.

To the students of The Daniel Academy —K.H. and K.H.

You are a living thing.
You breathe.

You eat.

You sleep.

You work and you play.

You have dreams and fears.

You have thoughts and memories.

You are.

You are someone's child.

You might have one parent or two.
You might have relatives who take care of you.
You might be adopted. No matter who your family is,
you deserve all the love you can get.

You are an animal.

You are a member of the mammal family. You have bones. You have hair. You drink milk. You are closely related to the chimpanzee.

Like all other animals, you call Earth home.

You are a body of water.

More than half of you is made of water. The water in your sweat cools you off. The water in your saliva helps you eat. The water in your blood helps carry nutrients to your body. Rivers flow through you.

**You are
an astronaut.**

You are a passenger
on a ship called Earth.
You sail around a star
called the sun. The sun
voyages through a galaxy
called the Milky Way.
You are always moving
through space.

You are a sponge.

You are constantly soaking
up new information. You
are a student of the world.
You learn by trying new
things. You absorb
everything you see,
hear, taste, smell,
and touch.

You are a friend.

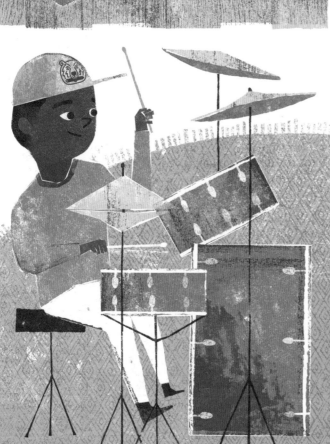

You are someone who likes to play with others.
Others also like to play with you.

You share.
You listen.

You care about how others feel.
You are someone others can count on.

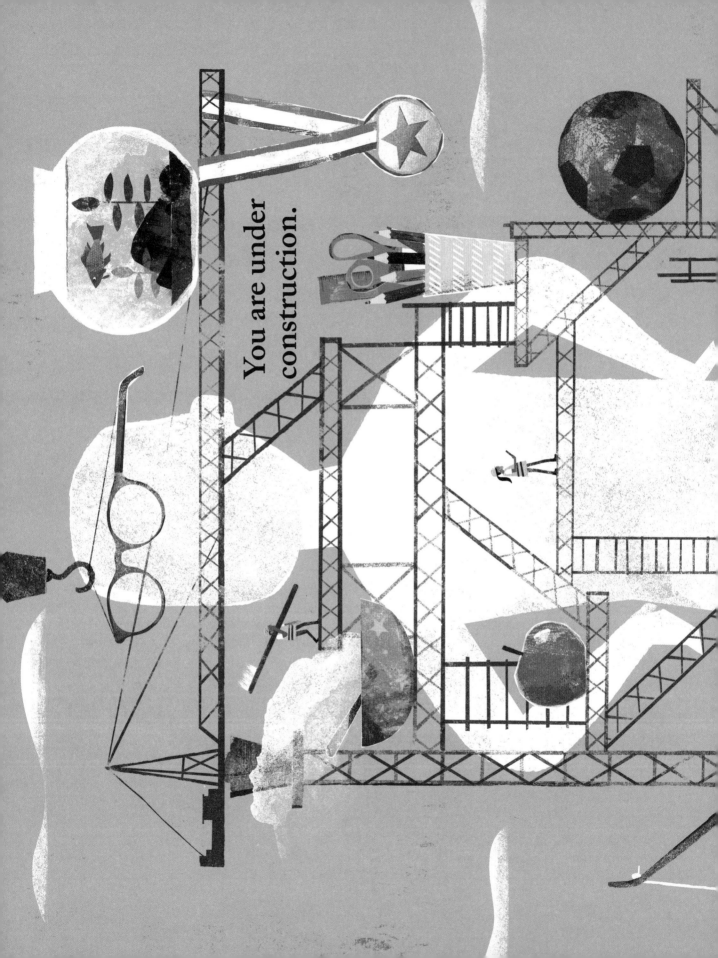

You are under construction.

You are not a finished person. You are a work in progress. You are growing, learning, and changing every day. Even when you grow up, you still won't be finished. Life is always building you.

You are a mystery.

What will you be when you grow up?
What will you look like?

Will you have children
of your own?

Where will you live?

Who will you live with? Nobody knows. Not even you.

You are one-of-a-kind.

Even if you are a twin, there is no one exactly like you.
There never has been another you. You are the only
you that will ever be. You cannot be copied.
You are unique. You are special.

You are a miracle.

You started out as one tiny cell inside another person. You split into two cells, then four, then eight. You grew into a baby. You pushed your way into the world. You became your own person.

You are a story.

You are the author of your life.
Every day is a blank page waiting for you
to fill it. Make your story funny. Make it
interesting. Make it an adventure.
Tell your story to others.

Then listen
to theirs.